GARFIELD'S GHOST STORIES

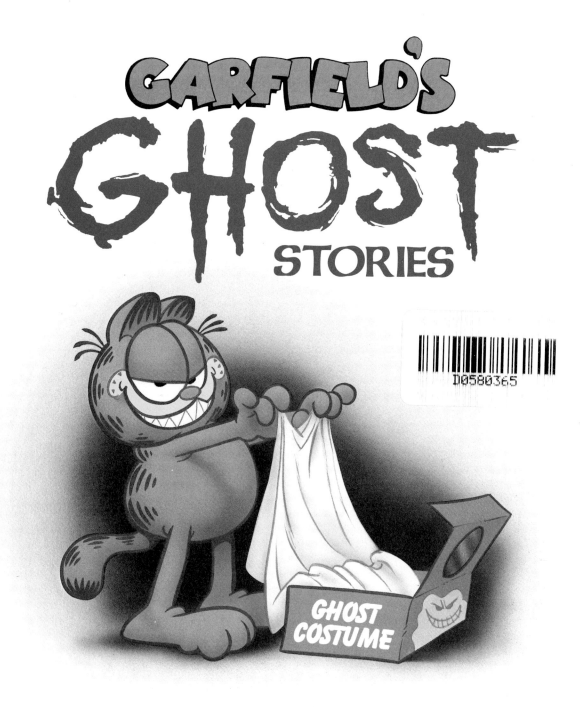

Created by

JIM DAVIS

Written by Mark Acey and Jim Kraft
Illustrated by Mike Fentz

PAWS, INC.

Watermill Press

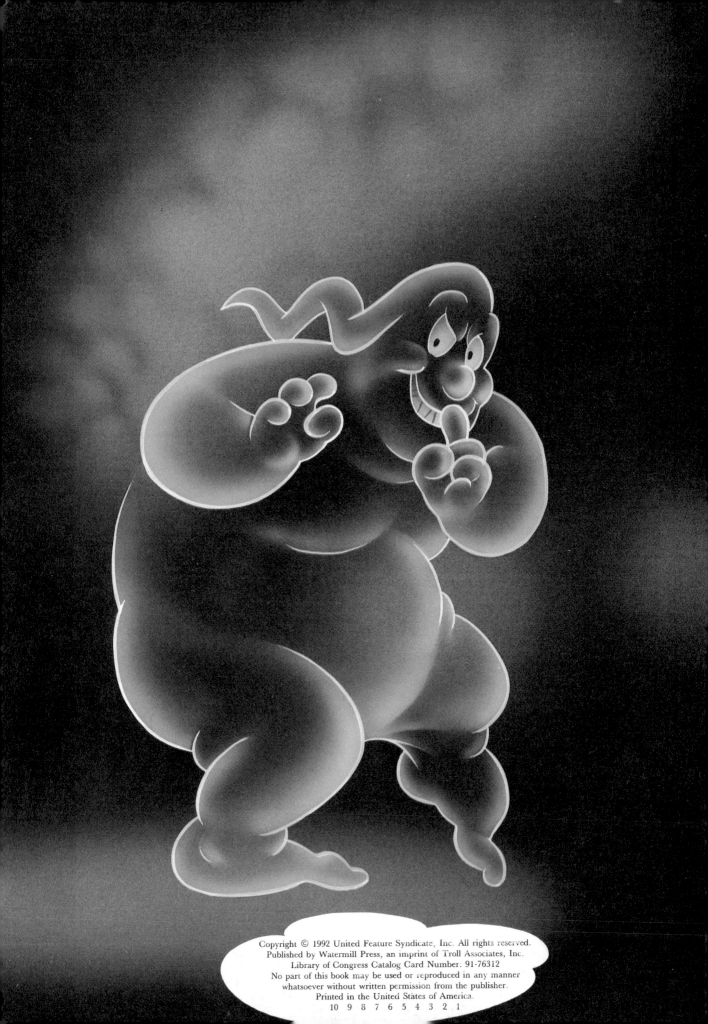

Contents

The Headless Pirate

"Yo ho ho!" roared Garfield as he swaggered across the room, brandishing a sword in Odie's direction. "Out of me way, you mangy sea dog, or I'll run you through with me cutlass. For I am Orangebeard, the most feared buccaneer ever to sail the seven seas!"

"GARFIELD! Put that thing down!" yelled Jon, rushing into the room. "That sword's a priceless family heirloom. It belonged to my great-great-great-great-great uncle, Shamus Arbuckle. Did I ever tell you about Uncle Shamus?"

"Oh no," moaned Garfield. "I sense another family anecdote coming on."

"Yessir," continued Jon. " 'Famous Shamus' they called him. He was the captain of the HMS *Pearl,* the ship that finally captured the notorious pirate Blackbeard back in 1718. And what a ferocious fight it was. It took twenty-five pistol-and-sword wounds to finish off the fierce pirate. Afterward, they put Blackbeard's head on a pole. And Uncle Shamus received Blackbeard's sword as a reward for his bravery."

"A hero in the Arbuckle family," marveled Garfield. "Will wonders never cease?"

"Now," added Jon, "before I go out tonight, I'm going to put the sword back in its case for safekeeping. And when I return, that sword had better be there."

Naturally, no sooner had Jon left than Garfield opened the case and grabbed the cutlass.

"Now, where were we, Odie?" asked Garfield mischievously. "Orangebeard craves action. Is there no man who braves a taste o' me cutlass? Where is that sissy Blackbeard?"

Suddenly the lights went out. A rumble shook the house and a cloud of smoke poured from the fireplace.

"By thunder!" boomed a mighty voice. "Who dares speak ill the name o' Blackbeard? Prepare to meet yer maker."

As the smoke cleared and the lights blinked on, Garfield and Odie could see the horrifying specter of a decapitated pirate holding his severed head.

"Be this the house of Arbuckle?" growled Blackbeard. "Speak up lads, or I'll cut out yer tongues and feed 'em to the fishes!"

"Don't lose your head," quipped Garfield. "Yes, this is the Arbuckle house. Do you like it? It's yours."

" 'Tis not a house I seek," snarled Blackbeard. " 'Tis me prized cutlass—and vengeance!"

Garfield gulped, then quickly slipped the cutlass behind his back.

"Fer the last three centuries, I been trackin' down relatives o' the crew who laid me low. Mind ye, fer that I bear them no harm. Takin' a man's head is fair, but stealin' his sword . . . aye, that's a different matter. And when I find the snake who holds me cutlass, vengeance will be mine."

With a hideous grunt, Blackbeard hoisted his severed head high into the air.

"An eye fer an eye and a head fer a head!" he roared. "Which brings me to Shamus Arbuckle."

"You mean 'Famous Shamus,' " said Garfield.

"Aye, so you heard of him," said Blackbeard. "Famous for his bad food he was. Worst cook ever to disgrace a ship's galley."

"You mean he wasn't a captain?" asked Garfield.

"A cap'n now? Hah! The only time that coward set foot on a deck was to swab it. But he could have lifted me sword after all the fightin' was done. And if'n he did, somebody in this house is goin' to pay!"

"So that explains it," thought Garfield. "A heroic Arbuckle . . . I should have known better."

"Where's me blasted cutlass?" Blackbeard shouted furiously.

He pounded the table with his fist, causing his severed head to drop to the floor and roll behind Garfield.

"AHA!" shrieked Blackbeard, spying the sword. "It's me cutlass! Say yer prayers, matey . . . yer not long fer this world!"

"That's our cue, Odie," yelled Garfield. "Run for it!"

But before they could move, the monstrous pirate snatched them up by their tails and dangled them over his gruesome head.

"Hand it over!" commanded Blackbeard.

"Hand what over?" asked Garfield.

Blackbeard bared his teeth and started to growl.

"Okay, okay," said Garfield. "Take it."

Heaving Garfield and Odie aside, Blackbeard grabbed the sword and began polishing it with care. He then picked up his head for a better look.

"Shiver me timbers!" he bellowed. "This is not me cutlass . . . it says 'Colonial Toy Makers.' What manner of mischief be this?"

"Elementary, my dear Blackbeard," replied Garfield. "Obviously Shamus was trying to impress people by pretending to have your sword. I guess he wanted to be famous for more than his cooking."

"Then where the devil is me cutlass?"

"Who knows?" said Garfield. "Maybe you should check all the army surplus stores. If you start now, you could finish by the year 3000. And while you're at it, you might consider picking up a bowling bag for your head."

Ranting and raving, Blackbeard tucked his head under his arm and disappeared in a puff of smoke.

Moments later Jon's car pulled into the driveway.

"Quick, Odie," said Garfield. "Put the sword back. And smudge over that inscription. What Jon doesn't know won't hurt him."

When Jon came in, he headed straight for the cutlass.

"Ah, it's still in the case," he said. "You boys haven't been playing with it, have you?"

"Us?" said Garfield. "Not a ghost of a chance."

Lady of the Mist

Fingers of mist floated off the mountain lake, creeping through the trees until they coiled around the log cabin where Garfield, Jon, and Odie sat staring at the fire in the hearth.

Jon sighed. "I'm really depressed tonight," he said. "Maybe it's this fog. Maybe it's because our vacation is nearly over."

"Maybe it's because any second we could be eaten by a bear," suggested Garfield.

"Being out here in the mountains, miles from other people—it makes me realize how lonely I am," Jon continued. "I mean, it's great to have pets. But I'm missing that one special person."

"Me, too," Garfield agreed. "It's the pizza delivery man."

Suddenly Odie jumped to his feet and began sniffing the air.

"What is it, Odie?" Jon whispered.

Giving a low growl, Odie pointed at the cabin door.

"Something's out there," said Garfield. "It could be a pet-eating bear."

There was a light knock at the door.

"A very *polite* pet-eating bear."

Jon unlocked the door and peeked outside. Then he swung the door wide open.

There in the mist stood a woman in a down jacket, jeans, and hiking boots.

"Sorry to bother you," she said softly, "but do you think I could stay here tonight?"

"Would you?" said Jon. "I mean, come in!"

The woman stepped inside. In the firelight her face looked very pale. Pale, but beautiful, Jon thought.

"I'm Jon Arbuckle," said Jon, extending his hand.

"Emily Webb," said the woman.

"Brrrr. Your hand is like ice," said Jon. "How long have you been out there?"

"Seems like forever," she replied. "I was trying to get back to my campsite. But I couldn't find it in this fog."

"You'll have no problem in the morning," Jon said. "But for now, I'll put another log on the fire. And get you a blanket. And make some hot chocolate."

While Jon was fussing around the cabin, his two pets introduced themselves to the stranger.

"I'm Garfield, and this is Odie," said Garfield. "We're glad you're not a bear. Got any snacks?"

"You have adorable pets, Jon," she said.

"They take after their owner," Jon replied.

"Odie, I think we've been insulted," said Garfield.

Jon brought the hot chocolate. He and Emily sat by the fire. They talked. Emily was a botanist studying the mountain flowers. She'd found some unusual specimens near the rim of Bottomless Gorge. The more she talked, the brighter became the gleam in Jon's eyes.

"Uh-oh," Garfield said to Odie. "Jon's got that 'happily ever after' look on his face again. I see a major rejection on the horizon."

It grew late. Jon insisted that Emily take the bed while he and his pets bedded down on the floor.

"You're very kind, Jon," said Emily.

"Then I wish he'd kindly stop hogging the covers," complained Garfield.

Under the blankets Jon whispered to his pets. "Am I a lucky guy or what? She's beautiful. She's intelligent. I think I've met the woman of my dreams!"

"And she's met the man of her nightmares," grumbled Garfield. "Go to sleep."

When they awoke the next morning, the mist had disappeared . . . and so had the woman.

Jon rushed outside. "Emily! Emily!" he called. There was no reply. "Where is she?" Jon cried. "We've got to find her!"

"I find better on a full stomach," Garfield reminded him.

"She must be hiking back to her camp," Jon decided. "Probably didn't want to bother me. Isn't she thoughtful? Come on! We'll take the car and catch her!"

Jon shoved Garfield and Odie into the car. They sped off, bumping and skidding on the dirt road. Suddenly they saw a ranger walking along the road ahead. Jon screeched to a halt.

"Have you seen a woman named Emily Webb?" Jon demanded. He described Emily to the ranger.

"Haven't seen her," said the ranger. "But neither have you, really."

"What do you mean?"

The ranger leaned on the car. "Emily Webb came here about five years ago to study the flowers. Nice lady. Smart lady. But one day she disappeared. We hunted for her a long time. Finally our helicopter spotted her body on a ledge in Bottomless Gorge. Guess she must have slipped. We tried, but we never could reach her. The ledge was too far down."

"But I saw her! Last night!" Jon blurted out.

"Oh, people do see her. On misty nights she sometimes stops by a cabin. Her spirit just gets lonely, I suppose. Anyway, now you can tell your grandkids that you've seen a ghost."

"Funny, she didn't look ghostish," said Garfield.

The ranger walked on, leaving Jon slumped over the wheel.

"Just my luck, I fell in love with a ghost," moaned Jon. "I'll never find that special someone. I'll always be alone."

Garfield and Odie looked at each other. "Alone? Don't be ridiculous," said Garfield. Then he and Odie gave Jon a big hug.

"Thanks, guys," said Jon. "I really needed that."

"Hey," replied Garfield, "what are pets for?"

The Well-Fed Phantom

Garfield peered through the iron gates at the run-down old house. "It doesn't look haunted to me," he said hopefully.

"It's haunted, all right," Nermal replied. "But I thought you weren't afraid of ghosts."

"I'm not afraid!" snapped Garfield. "I'll stay in that house all night or my name isn't Garfunkel."

"Your name *isn't* Garfunkel."

"Then I'm out of here!" said Garfield.

Nevertheless, a short time later Garfield was tiptoeing with a flashlight through the creepy old house. "Yech! It's a regular cobweb convention," Garfield whispered to himself. "Why did I let Nermal dare me into spending the night in a haunted house?"

Garfield's instincts guided him to the kitchen. At the sight of him, rats scurried into their holes. Garfield pulled a tattered rug in front of the dust-covered refrigerator and settled down for the night.

Hour after hour Garfield huddled against the fridge. The house creaked and shuddered, and every sound made Garfield jerk with fright. Suddenly he heard a fierce growl.

Garfield patted his empty tummy. "Why didn't I bring snacks?" he said, glancing around the dusty kitchen. Then he turned and stared at the grimy old refrigerator. "Hmm," he said. "I wonder . . ."

A short time later, as Garfield was falling asleep, a terrible voice rumbled in a far-off room.

"I'm coming to eat you up!" groaned the voice.

Garfield nearly jumped out of his stripes! "That's it. I'm leaving. I'm gone," he gasped. But his legs were paralyzed with fear!

"I'm coming to eat you up!" the voice repeated.

"Do you hear that, legs?" wailed Garfield, struggling to move.

The voice was getting closer and closer. "I'm coming to eat you up!" it rumbled. "I'm coming to eat you up!"

Suddenly the kitchen door burst open and in floated a well-fed phantom.

"AAAAAAH!" screamed Garfield.

"AAAAAAH!" shrieked the ghost, who immediately retreated behind the door. Seconds later his head popped back in.

"My goodness, kitty. You almost scared the after-life out of me."

"Don't eat me!" pleaded Garfield.

"Eat you?" the ghost replied. "Don't be ridiculous. I came down for my midnight snack. I'm sure there's something much tastier than you in the refrigerator."

"Uh-oh," said Garfield.

The ghost opened the refrigerator door and gasped. "It's empty!" he shrieked. "But it should be full! It's always been full!"

The ghost eyed Garfield angrily.

"Well, uh, being scared makes me hungry," Garfield explained. "So naturally I had to check the fridge and . . ."

"Then there's only one thing I can do," the ghost said gravely. "I'll have to eat—"

Garfield didn't wait for the ghost to finish. He ran all the way home—faster than a fat cat with a full tummy had ever run before.

The Haunted Pyramid

"What a great vacation!" exclaimed Jon to Garfield and Odie. "I can't believe we're actually standing inside an Egyptian pyramid!"

"I can't believe we actually rode a camel," groaned Garfield. "I'm going to be walking funny for a week."

"According to my guidebook," said Jon, "the pyramids were built as tombs for the rulers of Egypt, who were called pharaohs. We're inside the Great Pyramid, the largest of them all."

"Big deal," griped Garfield, pacing back and forth in the long stone passageway. "All this space and I haven't seen one hot-dog stand yet."

"There's more," continued Jon. "It says here that the pharaoh Khufu was buried inside this pyramid along with precious objects such as gold, jewels, and even a sacred cat. The Egyptians worshiped cats."

"Obviously an advanced civilization," said Garfield.

"But get this," said Jon excitedly. "Legend has it that Khufu's cat was stolen shortly after his burial. And ever since the theft, Khufu's vengeful spirit has been stalking this pyramid, forever roaming and searching, unable to find peace until he finds his long-lost cat."

Jon closed the book and cringed.

"Ooh, that's some spooky story. Who knows? . . . Khufu's spirit could be watching us right now." Jon walked farther into the tunnel, with Odie tagging along behind him.

"All I know," said Garfield, "is that my growling stomach's not going to find peace until I find a snack shop. I'm history."

And with that, Garfield set off in the opposite direction to search for food. Up one corridor he went, then down another . . . this way, that way, through another puzzling passageway . . . until at last he found himself in the deepest, darkest recesses of the pyramid.

"Uh-oh," gulped Garfield, obviously lost. "Something tells me I zigged when I should have zagged. What am I going to do now? If I don't get back soon, Jon is going to kill me."

Suddenly Garfield heard an eerie hissing sound.

"What was that?" he murmured.

The sound grew louder. Someone—or some*thing*—was getting closer . . . closer . . . and closer! Garfield's heart began beating faster . . . faster . . . and faster! The hissing had now become a fierce growl. Numb with fear, Garfield turned to face the unseen menace. What he saw were two piercing red eyes, glowing in the darkness.

"You know, you ought to get more sleep," said Garfield. "It'd do wonders for those bloodshot eyes and you'd be a lot less cranky."

"Silence!" thundered the unearthly voice. "I am the spirit of Khufu. Who dares invade my royal chamber? If thou art a thief, thou shalt surely die!"

Suddenly there was a flash of light and Garfield could see the scowling phantom of a pharaoh. He could also see a strange look come over the pharaoh's ghostly face.

"AHA!" bellowed Khufu. "At last I have found thee! Come to me, my sacred cat!"

"Say what?" replied Garfield. "Have we met . . . maybe at a Halloween party?"

"Thou art Khatfu, the royal feline. I am Khufu, thy master. For thousands of years—since grave robbers stole thee away—I have waited for this moment. Now, through a miracle, thou hast returned to me. At last my spirit can rest."

"That's quite a tale," said Garfield. "It'd make a great movie of the week. Unfortunately, I'm not your cat. My name's Garfield and—"

"Enough!" shouted Khufu. "I command thee to come hither."

"I know I'll hate myself for asking, but what exactly do you have in mind?"

"Thou shalt be mummified and together our spirits shall spend all eternity."

"Gee, that's nice of you to offer," said Garfield, "but I think I'm all booked up for eternity. Besides, I don't look good in bandages."

Khufu was not amused. He lunged at Garfield. Garfield jumped away and started to run. "Guess it's time for the chase scene."

Through the pyramid he fled, veering and swerving at breakneck speed with Khufu in hot pursuit. Finally Garfield barreled around a corner and crashed into the statue of a sphinx. Sprawled helplessly on the floor, he looked up and saw the angry Khufu hovering over him.

"Looks like I'm a goner," moaned Garfield, clutching at the statue. "And I didn't even get a last meal."

Suddenly the statue pivoted, revealing a space under the floor.

"A secret compartment!" gasped Garfield. "Smashing into the statue must have caused it to open. And look—there's a box with my picture on it!"

"So that's where Ghoofu put it!" shrieked Khufu.

"Who?" asked Garfield. "And what *is* that thing?"

"Khatfu's coffin," explained Khufu. "My faithful but stupid servant, Ghoofu, put Khatfu's mummy in the wrong place! I should have remembered Ghoofu could never do anything right. What an imperial imbecile I am!"

"Don't be too hard on yourself," said Garfield. "The memory's always the first thing to go. And speaking of going, now that Khatfu has been returned to his master, I've got to get back before *my* master has a fit."

"It is done," pronounced Khufu.

And with a wave of Khufu's hand, Garfield was magically transported back to Jon and Odie.

"There you are," snapped Jon. "It's about time. Now let's get going. Odie and I are dying to see the mummies."

Upon hearing that, Garfield turned white as a sheet and fainted.

"What's with him?" remarked Jon. "You'd think he'd just seen a ghost."

Terror in the Mirror

Lightning crackled across the black sky, filling the room with an eerie glow. Seconds later a clap of thunder shook the house and jolted Garfield from his sleep.

"Huh?!" blurted Garfield, nearly jumping out of his skin. "Oh, it's thunder," he added groggily. "For a minute I thought Odie was burping in his sleep again. Oh well, as long as I'm up, I might as well grab a snack."

Garfield turned on the light, squinted, and stumbled toward the kitchen. On his way he caught a glimpse of himself in the mirror. Suddenly he stopped dead in his tracks. Peering into the mirror, he saw a terrifying sight.

"AYIEEE!" screamed Garfield. "My fur! I've heard of bad haircuts, but this is ridiculous!"

Horrified, Garfield frantically ran his paw over his body. But he didn't feel anything unusual. He looked down and saw that he was all right.

"Whew!" he sighed. "Looks like I can cancel the fur transplant. But what's going on? Am I cracking up, or has this mirror just escaped from the *Twilight Zone*?"

Garfield rubbed his bleary eyes and leaned forward for a second look. This time, to his enormous relief, he saw what he usually saw—a fat furry cat.

"Ah, mirror, mirror, on the wall . . . I'm still the cutest of them all," crowed Garfield.

But then he noticed something else in the mirror, something looming behind his reflection. Looking closer, he could see a ghostly figure in white wielding a chain saw. And it was coming his way!

Garfield whirled around, but the room was empty. Then he turned back to the mirror for another look, only to meet the rampaging phantom crashing through the glass.

"Uh-oh," thought Garfield, diving out of the way. "Something tells me the fur is going to be flying."

"There's more than one way to skin a cat," howled the phantom as he cranked up his roaring chain saw. "But this way's the funnest!"

Garfield's eyes widened, his pulse quickened, his heart pounded, but there was no escaping the ghost. Cornered, Garfield could only lie helplessly against the wall and watch as the grinning specter crept ever closer. Finally the crazed phantom thrust the vibrating chain saw toward him. Garfield gasped—then lunged at the ghostly attacker.

A bloodcurdling cry pierced the air. But it was not Garfield screaming—nor was it his attacker.

It was Jon!

"Owww! Let go of my head, you crazy cat!" yelled Jon, as he pried Garfield loose. "What in the world has gotten into you? One minute you're napping and the next minute you're pouncing on me."

Garfield quickly scanned the room. There was no ghost and there was no mirror. It had all been a dream—a grisly, ghastly nightmare.

"Anyway," said Jon, "I just came in to remind you that it's almost time for that TV miniseries we've been watching, *Chain Saw Veterinarian*. I knew you wouldn't want to miss it."

"If you think I'm watching any more of that show," gasped Garfield, "then *you're* the one who's dreaming!"